MW00953273

WELCOME TO

I SPY

VALENTINE'S DAY

BOOK FOR KIDS AGES 2-5

THIS BOOK BELONGS TO:

_ _ _ _ _ _ _ _ _ _ _ _ _

I Spy Valentine's Day Book For Kids
Copyright © 2023 By Darya Dyes
All Rights Reserved.

I spy with my little eye something starting with ...

A is for Angel

I spy with my little eye something starting with ...

B is for Box

I spy with my little eye something starting with ...

C is for Chocolate

I spy with my little eye something starting with ...

D is for Dog

I spy with my little eye something starting with ...

E is for envelope

Be My

VaLentine

I spy with my little eye something beggining with

F is for Flowers

I spy with my little eye something beggining with

G is for Gnome

I spy with my little eye something starting with ...

H is for Heart

I spy with my little eye something starting with ...

i *is for Impala*

I spy with my little eye something starting with ...

J is for Jelly

I spy with my little eye something starting with ...

K is for King

I spy with my little eye something starting with ...

monkey LOVE

sweet heart

be mine

L is for Love birds

I spy with my little eye something starting with ...

M is for Moon

I spy with my little eye something starting with ...

N is for Night time

I spy with my little eye something starting with ...

O is for Owls

I spy with my little eye something beggining with

P is for perfume

I spy with my little eye something starting with ...

Q is for Queen

I spy with my little eye something starting with ...

R is for Rose

I spy with my little eye something starting with ...

S is for sweets

I spy with my little eye something starting with ...

T is for Teddy bear

I spy with my little eye something starting with ...

U is for Unicorn

I spy with my little eye something starting with ...

V is for Valentine

I spy with my little eye something starting with ...

W

Happy Valentine's Day

W is for Wings

I spy with my little eye something starting with ...

X is for Xylophone

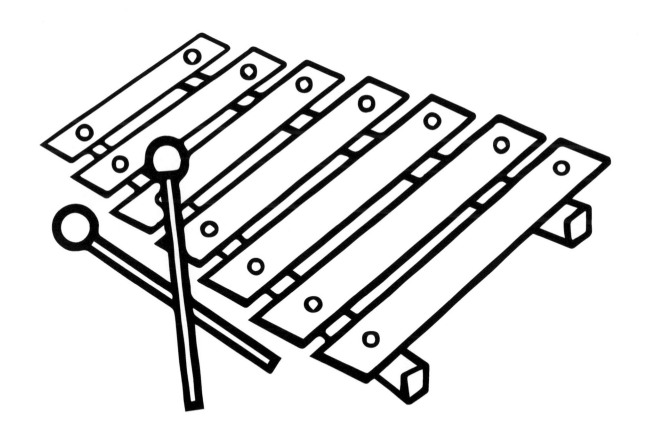

I spy with my little eye something starting with ...

Y is for Yarn

I spy with my little eye something starting with ...

Z is for Zebra

Made in the USA
Las Vegas, NV
02 February 2023

66734893R00059